# The Day Leo Said
# I HATE YOU!

By Robie H. Harris          Illustrated by Molly Bang

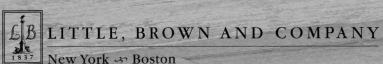
LITTLE, BROWN AND COMPANY
1837
New York · Boston

Today, Leo's mommy couldn't stop saying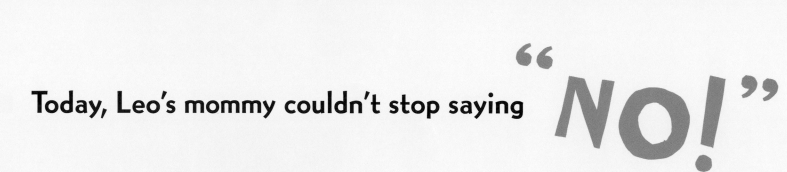

"No rolling tomatoes across the floor!" she said.

in the
fishbowl!"

 "**NO** dancing on the table!"

 "**NO** squeezing toothpaste down the toilet!"

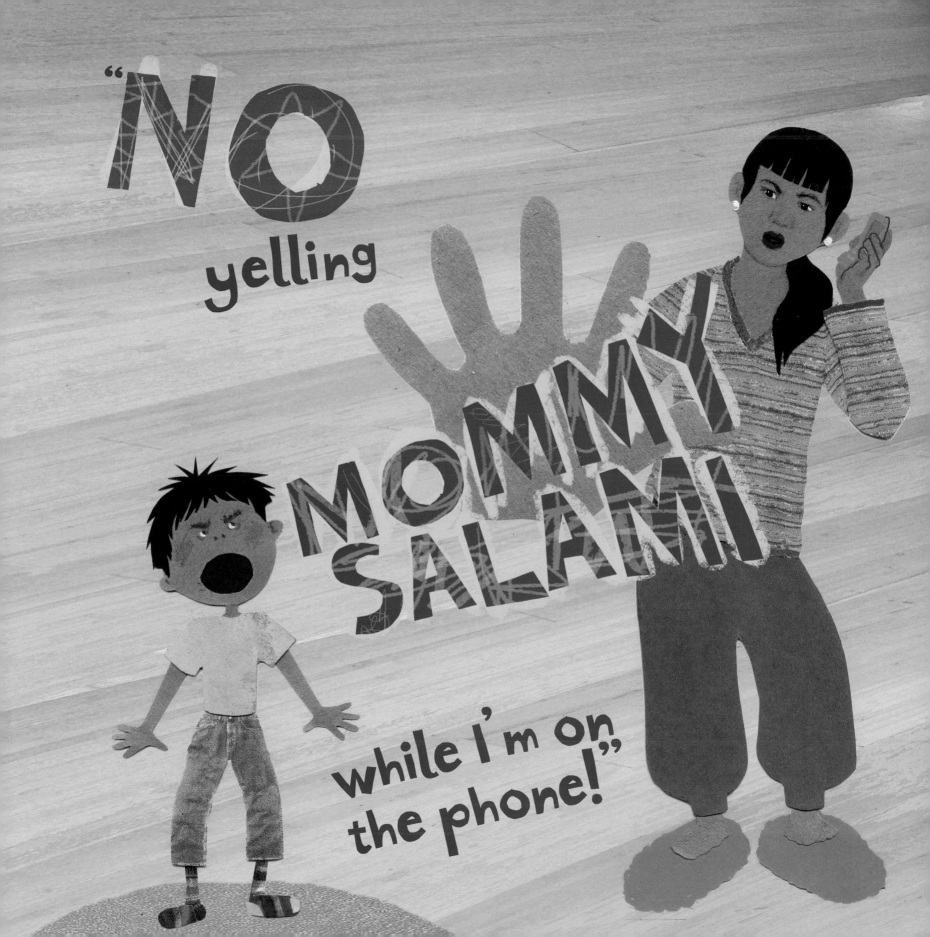

"Mommy, no more NO's! I HATE no!"

Leo told her.

"Leo," she said, "I know you hate no. But there are some things you just should not do."

"Then I'm going to my room where **nobody** can say

NO

Leo took out his crayons.
He drew a picture.
On his wall.

Of Mommy!

He made her mouth turn down.
He made her hair stick way up in the air.

Leo threw his crayons down.

"You can't say **NO** in my room!" he yelled.

"So Mommy, go to your room and stay there — for one hundred whole days!"

But Mommy didn't go anywhere at all. "Sometimes," she said, "I **have** to say NO!"

"But I **HATE NO!**" shouted Leo.

"And actually, really right now—

Leo wanted to stuff "I HATE YOU!" right back in his mouth.

But it was too late.  The words popped out before he could stop them.

Mommy took a deep breath.

"**WHAT** did you just say?"

she said very slowly.

"Well . . ." Leo muttered,
"last night . . . you said . . .

'I **hate** broccoli!'"

"BROCCOLI?"

bellowed Mommy.

"Broccoli ..." Leo mumbled.

"I am NOT broccoli!
You are NOT broccoli!"

hollered Mommy.

"I can hate broccoli.
You can hate broccoli!
We even can say,
I hate broccoli!

But saying 'I hate you!'—
to anybody—

can make people feel
really bad!"

"Mommy?" asked Leo.

"Do you . . . hate me . . . for saying,

I hate you?"

"I hated it when you said those three words to me. But Leo, I could never ever hate you—

because I love you."

"Whew!" Leo sighed. And he reached up and hugged Mommy.

"But . . ." she said.
"But what?" he asked.

"But I still hate broccoli!" Mommy said.

"I hate smelly cheese," said Leo.
"I hate sand between my toes!" said Mommy.
"I hate it when I have a runny nose!" said Leo.
"I hate it when I have a runny nose, too!"
said Mommy.

"Well," said Leo, "I don't think you will hate this!"

Leo grabbed a pad of paper.
He picked up a crayon.

"Mommy, close your eyes!" he said.

And she did.

Leo drew a new picture of Mommy.

He drew a smile on her face and a pretty purple flower
in her up-in-the-air hair.
And when Mommy opened her eyes—
she loved what she saw.

And so did Leo.